Murder on a Yacht

Penelope Sotheby

~~~

Paperback Edition

Free Book

Sign up for this author's new release mailing list and receive a free copy of her very first novella *Murder At The Inn*. This fantastic whodunit will keep you guessing to the very end and is not currently available anywhere else.

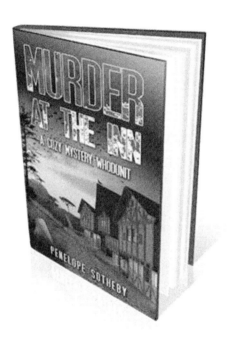

Other Books By The Author

Table Of Contents

Chapter 1

Apple Mews would normally be characterized by any outsider as quiet, like a strictly-guarded library. And for those outsiders who pass through on a scenic Sunday drive, their minds might, for a fleeting moment, yearn for such a peaceful life. Mind you, these passing whimsies are probably made without the knowledge that Apple Mews has in fact been associated with more than one murder.

But besides that point, it is fairly safe to conclude that all who call it home are happy they live in the Shropshire village.

Still, although Apple Mews only has a couple hundred households, the serene semblance can be quite deceiving. For when you meet the villagers, you'll soon learn that many have boisterous quirks or behaviours, loud both in terms of volume and eccentricity.

At this very moment, in fact, some of Apple Mews' primary school students are up to their regular pranks. Three boys, aged 10 and 11, are kneeling on Mrs. Oakley's front walkway. The focus of their attention are the bottles just delivered by the milkman. The ringleader of the pranksters, Tommy Turner, pulls out a small bottle of blue food colouring. Snickering, while being egged on by his mates, he removes the cap from one of the milk bottles. Less than a second before young Tommy squeezes a drop of blue into the milk, he is stopped by a—

"HALT!"

Tommy drops the food colouring – on the ground, not in the bottle of milk – and looks around.

"Did you hear something?" he asks his mates.

His accomplices nod their heads and shrug their shoulders at the same time. It definitely sounded like a grownup lady's voice, but the only people they see are younger pupils running in the opposite direction up the road.

Tommy picks up the food colouring from the ground.

"HALT!" Diane Dimbleby yells once again, and immediately ducks for cover below her windowsill. She bites her finger to contain her laughter. Staying hidden, she shouts even louder to ensure she's still heard, "You will immediately replace the milk cap, run home as fast as you can and return the blue food colouring to your mother!"

Tommy's accomplices move their heads in every direction, searching for the source of the commanding voice. Tommy, stunned, does not move a muscle.

Diane slowly raises her eyes above the windowsill, and yells "MOVE!"

The boys do not need another warning. Tommy quickly replaces the milk cap, stands and sprints away, even faster than his mates, without looking back.

Once all the boys are out of sight, Diane finally allows herself to release the stream of laughter she had barely contained.

"I've still got it!" she says amusingly to herself, referring to her former years teaching at the same school these boys now attend. Her specialty had been dealing with the eldest, most rambunctious pupils – truth be told she got a kick out of their mischief, although she would never reveal this to her classes.

Diane had taught at Apple Mews' up until a few years ago. Now in her sixties and retired, she is still working, but in another field. Perhaps it was an odd concept some years ago, but for Diane, it had been her plan all along. While teaching had been a passion, she still had to bow to the exigencies of school administrators, parents, and curriculum outcomes. Now, however, she is free to work at her own pace and with creative liberty, doing what she loves best: writing and editing books.

Diane walks next door, collects the milk bottles and walks up to Mrs. Oakley's front door. Immediately after Diane knocks, Mrs. Oakley comes out to the porch.

"I wouldn't have much minded drinking blue milk, but I'm very grateful that you intervened," Mrs. Oakley smiles.

"Ah, you're a good sport Mrs. Oakley!" Diane giggles.

"Won't you come in for a cuppa?"

"I thank you kindly, but I really must finish getting ready for my weekend getaway. Are you sure you don't mind taking care of Rufus in my absence?"

"Not at all my dear! He's good company," Mrs. Oakley responds. "He'll protect me and my milk!"

Diane thanks her neighbour and returns home to finish packing for her trip. Her long-time friend,

Mike Davies, has invited her to spend the weekend on the Island of Lundy, which is off the North Devon coast. Lundy is a beautiful isle with a rich and long history, but it is endowed with a variety of reputations.

Some say that it's a drunkard's paradise – the after-hour parties, organized by the thrill seekers who visit the island for scuba diving and climbing excursions, are rumoured to get quite rowdy. On the other hand, some describe Lundy as the most peaceful place on Earth – a haven for birdwatching, serene walks and waking up to the sunrise, not the alarm clock. Still others say it's the perfect place for writers and artists to find inspiration.

Diane, who has visited her friend Mike and Lundy at least three or four times, has not yet decided how she would describe the island. Each time she goes though, it is a welcome change from the hullabaloo that even the small village of Apple Mews seems to generate. On every visit, she makes sure to walk along the beach and enjoy a delicious seafood meal at the island's tavern.

Her friend Mike owns an impressive forty-foot yacht which, during the summer and autumn months, he docks as much as he can at the Lundy Island pier. Each time he invites Diane for a visit, he welcomes her to stay aboard his yacht too.

In recent years, however, Diane's sea legs have become wobblier and she does not enjoy sailing like she used to. She prefers to stay on *terra-firma* as much as possible, or at least while she sleeps. She had proposed a compromise: "I will join you as you sail around the Bristol Channel on Saturday

4

and Sunday, but this time I will spend the night at the Puffin's Nest," she had told him. She has booked the B&B's especially cosy loft bedroom for this trip.

Diane had assured herself that she could handle the daytime on the boat. Their conversations – which never go dry because of their long-time friendship and mutual admiration for reading and writing – would distract her if the waves got too choppy.

Mike of course agreed to the suggested compromise, because he knew that would be the only way that his dear friend would agree to come visit.

Mike is not quite a hermit, but is on the cusp of becoming one. Since retiring from the MI6 – for those not familiar with the world of undercover operations, MI6 is the common name for Britain's Secret Intelligence Service – the 63-year-old native Londoner has taken refuge on his yacht. He likes to keep to himself. In fact, wherever he travels, he's more likely to stay the night on his boat rather than in a hotel.

Those who don't know Mike Davies well would call him shy or aloof. One might conclude that a former MI6 spy has to be that way, living a secretive life and all. *"...the secrecy of our operations and the identity of those who work with us is our foremost principle..."* Perhaps not being able to talk about past covert operations – even traumas – makes getting close to anyone increasingly difficult.

Of course, many readers have had a chance to gain a slight glimpse of insight into the life of Mike Davies. The published author's novels, although works of fiction, are inspired by his intelligence days and even describe some factual events.

And those lucky enough to be a friend of Mike's know that he is as loyal as they come. Diane is one of these lucky few and knows that if she were ever in a pickle, she could turn to him for help. Yet it seems that this time, it is Mike that may need help.

Earlier this Saturday morning, before, as they say, the rooster crowed, Diane drove to Ifracombe as the crow flies. Now crossing the Bristol Channel, aboard the ferry to Lundy Island, she thinks of the conversation she'd had with Mike when he asked her to come for the weekend. She remembers thinking the invitation seemed almost desperate. It was not what he said, but the simplicity of the words he used: it was an earnest request – "Please come." Diane has the sense they will be discussing more than just his latest spy novel.

As the ferry nears Lundy Island's dock, Diane can easily make out the familiar, ghost-white, full head of hair atop her slightly tall friend. She eagerly waves and Mike reciprocates with a basic yet warm salute.

He walks up to the gangway to personally assist Diane off the boat, even though she is very agile for her age, and regardless of the fact that the gangway is easy to manoeuvre. Still, Diane obligingly takes his hand and even allows him to take her valise.

Both standing on the wharf, Mike quickly takes Diane in his arms and gives her a big hug. Although the two friends have been communicating often lately, it must be a year since Diane has visited the island and her friend.

Mike is pleased to see Diane, who is all smiles. The two go back 60 years and have always been comfortable with one another. Although they grew up in different places – Mike in London and Diane in Apple Mews – their two families were friends and got together often. Diane remembers that when they were little, the two shared a boundless imagination and often concocted such elaborate games, like complex treasure hunts or adventures in fantastical worlds.

Now, 60 years later, they find themselves at a place that could be described as just as magical. Together they walk to the Puffin's Nest B&B, so Diane can check in and drop off her suitcase. As they walk up the trail bisecting the moorland of purple heather, Mike comments on the last week's weather, the birth of a new Lundy pony and the latest artist-in-residence.

"She's working on a collection of paintings that simultaneously reflect the island's ecology above and below water. I'm looking forward to seeing them."

Mike stops and looks off in the distance. He holds his binoculars up to his eyes and nods his head. He removes the strap from around his neck and passes the binoculars to Diane.

"Look over there," he says, pointing. "Some of the island's feral goat population.

Diane focuses the lenses until the furry creatures with their pronounced, slightly curled horns come into focus. She slowly moves her body 360 degrees to scan the rest of the landscape. She marvels at the tall brick lighthouse, and then the climbers scaling a vertical granite cliff above a torrent of crashing waves, and then what just might be a colony of puffins way off in the distance.

Still looking through the binoculars, Diane is nearly toppled over by two children sprinting past. Diane laughs at the excited youngsters, as their parents, following behind, apologize.

"Not to worry," says Diane. "It's so refreshing to see children playing outside instead of trapped indoors with their eyes glued to a screen."

"They must be looking for letterboxes," Mike explains.

Lundy Island has numerous letterboxes scattered about. With a map in hand, those up for the challenge can try to find and collect a stamp from each, while solving riddles along the way.

"It sounds like we would have enjoyed that when we were kids," says Diane.

"Who are you kidding? You'd enjoy that now," chuckles Mike.

Inside the bed & breakfast, they are greeted by what seems to be an explosion of puffin knick-knacks, ornaments and curios. Clocks, figurines, plush toys, pictures, cushions and curtains all boast the black and white and orange colours of the seabird of which the accommodation is named after.

"Hello there Mike!" says a woman who runs out from behind an old-fashioned secretary desk cluttered with a puffin bobbleheads, mugs and postcards. "And you must be Diane Dimbleby! Welcome to the Puffin's Nest!"

The proprietor, a Mrs. Poole, does not even wait for Diane to show any proof of payment, but quickly ushers her upstairs to the loft. As fast as Mrs. Poole ran up the stairs, she runs out of the room and back downstairs.

Diane is immediately happy with her decision to stay at the B&B. The sun shining through the south-facing and ceiling windows invite her into the space that has a bed, a desk and private bathroom. Unlike the main floor – there is not a puffin in sight – several vibrant, potted plants add to the welcoming ambience of the room.

Mrs. Poole returns with a tray of scones and iced tea and urges Diane to make herself at home.

"Oh, there's a terrace!" says Diane excitedly, pointing to the small patio adjoined to her top-level room. "Shall we enjoy our snack outside?"

Diane slides open the screen door and Mike carries their tray outside. They each take a seat on a patio chair, content to be the target of the sun's rays.

"I'm so glad to be in your presence Diane on this beautiful day," says Mike, eyes closed.

"And I am happy to be here," says Diane. "But Mike, you must truly tell me why you invited me on this particular occasion. I have a feeling it's more than just to catch up. We've already been talking so much lately"

Mike does not say anything for several minutes. He stares down at the same children from earlier who are now posing next to a letterbox they have just found. Their mother snaps several pictures.

"I didn't want to say anything on the phone," he says finally. "But something's got me spinning. I needed to tell somebody about it. You were the first person that came to mind. I can trust you."

It is about his latest manuscript, Mike explains. He's received some menacing letters and threatening phone calls.

"Someone does not want my book to be published," he says softly.

"But it hasn't been published yet!" says a surprised Diane.

"But I have sent the pages to the publisher," says Mike.

Diane could understand if he received such attention once the book is on the bookshelves– this happened with many controversial books. But how could the contents of the book be leaked at this stage? Only the small team at the publishing house has read the manuscript. Mike would have sent his draft to them via e-mail as was customary these days, rather than sending a hard copy.

"Except they asked me to print the final version and send it to them by post."

This is most curious, Diane thinks. Is Mike being watched? Could a hacker somehow access the documents on Mike's computer? Has somebody bugged the publishing house? Did some fanatic at the post office even cunningly read Mike's pages?

"Do you think it's serious… the threats, I mean?" asks Diane.

Mike doesn't say a word. If Diane could read his mind, she would know he is wondering if he went too far this time. He's never written a "tell-all" autobiography about his time with the MI6 before, but he does tend to recall details from actual events in his novels. Not only does this make the stories more enticing for his readers, it's also been therapeutic for him – a way for him to process what had been a rollercoaster of a profession.

One of the most troubling moments of his career happened at what had been a celebration for others – a time when families and loved ones and a country was reunited. But something happened then that Mike has never been able to get over. He wrote about it in this latest novel – something that perhaps the British government nor the intelligence agency does not want revealed, not even under the guise of fiction.

"The MI6 is not a temporary employer," Mike whispers. "Once you've served under their flag, they will never let you be free to move on with your life."

"Sorry, did you say something Mike?" Diane asks.

"I said, let's go sailing!"

Chapter 2

Even for someone like Diane who does not feel so carefree aboard a ship anymore, today is the perfect day to be sailing around the Bristol Channel. The waters are relatively calm and have a particularly alluring hue, the winds are just the right intensity to fill the boat's sails, and the sun is shining at the most welcoming blaze.

"It's a perfect day for this, Mike," smiles Diane, tucking a grey lock behind her ear. "Thank you."

"Look over there," Mike says.

He's pointing to a handful of grey seals basking atop the rocks near the shore. Close to them, another seal emerges, only exposing its head above the water. Diane watches for some time to see where the head will pop up next. When she squints she can barely make out its whiskers.

Mike steers the ship away from shore into more open waters and drops anchor, so the two friends can enjoy a picnic of sausage rolls and sandwiches and tarts Mrs. Poole from the Puffin's Nest so generously packed them. Mike contributes two mugs and a bottle of sparkling white to the mix.

"If you don't mind terribly, I'd like you to show me those dreadful letters," says Diane after swallowing a morsel of salmon salad sandwich.

Mike continues looking out at the water as if he did not hear Diane's request. Diane decides she'd better not press the issue and instead stands up to stretch her fingers down to her toes.

After a few minutes, Mike gets up and goes down to his cabin. *Oh dear, I've upset him,* thinks Diane.

But her friend returns carrying some pages, the tri-folded creases clearly worn as if they had been opened and closed, read and re-read many times. When Mike passes the pages to Diane, she realizes she had been expecting them to have words formulated from the proverbial letters cut out of a magazine... and maybe even graphic images suggesting violence is near.

Instead they are simply typed, in all caps, in what looks like Times New Roman, size 12. One of the letters says:

"DEAR MIKE DAVIES, KINDLY WITHDRAW YOUR LATEST MANUSCRIPT OR ELSE YOUR DAYS ARE NUMBERED."

The other says:

"THIS IS YOUR LAST WARNING. CANCEL THE BOOK DEAL BEFORE IT'S TOO LATE FOR YOU."

The use of simple font and the absence of shock-value visuals makes the messages even more compelling, Diane thinks. She does not like what these menacing messages are suggesting. In her first-hand experience, and also writing about criminals, she knows there are some people so deranged and so malevolent that they like to torment and frighten their victims before committing the final, dirty deed. They enjoy delivering mental and emotional torture before going in for the *kill*.

"I can see why you've been concerned, Mike," says Diane quietly. And then with more gusto, she says, "Don't you worry. We're going to figure this all out."

When they return to shore, Diane does not take notice of the tourists walking along the beach or the family of ponies grazing up on the hill or the newlywed couple stamping their booklet at a nearby letterbox. All she can think about, all she can wonder, is if her friend really is in trouble or if some person with a disturbing sense of humour is just playing games. And besides, who aside from she and the people working at the publishing house know about Mike's book? With Big Brother watching and the assorted ways for strangers to spy via physical and virtual means, maybe a good deal more people have read her friend's, the retired MI6 agent, manuscript.

Diane takes out her mobile and stares at its screen.

"Mike, is there a phone I can use? My mobile isn't getting any bars."

"Yes, service is spotty on the island," says Mike. "You can use the phone at the tavern."

"Oh goodie! I was hoping to have a meal there tonight."

They walk the short distance to the tavern, called The Granite, which has a sterling reputation, and not just among Lundy Island residents and regulars. Visitors from Devon County and beyond will often make the trip to The Granite for dinner. And more than one London reviewer has said the island pub serves the best fish and seafood in England – Diane would have to agree.

She and Mike are welcomed by The Granite's landlord, Mr. Wilson, standing behind the bar. He's been chatting with someone sitting on bar stool, a fisherman and regular patron from the other side of the channel.

"Hello Mike! And welcome back, Mrs. Dimbleby!"

"Mr. Wilson, how do you remember every single guest who has ever frequented your tavern? It's uncanny," says Diane.

"Ah, it's not every visitor… just the ones worth remembering," Mr. Wilson winks.

"You sure know how to make a lady feel good," says Diane. "Now before I tuck into one of your nice meals, may I use your telephone briefly?"

"By all means, Mrs. Dimbleby, as long as you're not ringing Australia!"

"No sir, not quite that far," Diane laughs.

Mr. Wilson obligingly places the phone on top of the bar in front of Diane. She feels a heart-warming nostalgia as she stares down at the rotary telephone. She has to take a moment to think of the number she's about to dial. In more recent years, she's more familiar with memorizing the positions of numbers on the keypad rather than the numbers themselves. Once she deciphers the actual digits she'll need to 'spin', Diane dials.

"Detective Darrell Crothers," says the voice on the other end of the line.

"Hello, Darrell… it's—"

"Diane? Hello! We haven't spoken since your friend… Mrs. Jones… I meant to get in touch…"

"And me too… and now it seems I need your help."

Inspector Darrell Crothers of the Shrewsbury Police Station – the station responsible for a significant section of Shropshire, including Apple Mews – is a close friend of Diane's. The paths of the retired school teacher and the detective, now in his late 30s, have crossed on several occasions. All of these occasions have had one thing in common – murder. And although at times it causes Darrell to feel great anxiety, Diane normally finds a way to be of great assistance in solving said murders. It's no wonder that she's got a knack for writing murder mysteries. On this occasion however, Diane is asking for Darrell's assistance instead of offering it.

Diane turns her back to Mr. Wilson and the fisherman at the bar so they cannot hear, and tells the inspector all about her friend Mike Davies and the threatening letters and calls he's been receiving because of his manuscript. Diane knows that Darrell has the resources and know-how to assist in this investigation… before it's too late.

"Well, you caught me right before I was going on a two-day fishing holiday," says Darrell. "I suppose if your friend Mike is willing to take me sailing I would be willing to change my plans and come to Lundy to take a look at those letters."

"Oh thank you, Darrell! Thank you most kindly!"

Diane turns around and gives Mike a thumbs up. Mike lifts his shoulders, confused. He's unsure of who Diane is even talking to.

After Diane hangs up the phone, she and Mike sit down at a table near a window with an ample view of the sea. The wooden table is bare of any decorative pieces which is just fine, as the quality of cuisine – prepared by Mr. Wilson's wife and son – and the people who visit the tavern are more than enough to make the atmosphere most pleasing.

"I called my friend, Inspector Darrell Crothers…to help," explains Diane.

"But, I'm not sure Diane if we should involve anybody at this point," Mike, slightly protests. "Can we trust him?"

"Don't you worry, Mike. He's got a good head on his shoulders, this one."

Mr. Wilson takes Mike and Diane's dinner orders after serving them a couple pints of local brew. As they wait for their meals, more people trickle in to the tavern. A man, whose grey hair is mostly covered by his beige Tilley hat, is now sitting at the bar next to the fisherman. Diane recognizes him from at least one past visit.

"Who is that?" whispers Diane.

"Oh that's Shaun Boyle, the island's head marine conservationist," says Mike. "Nice chap."

Mr. Boyle's striking Irish accent makes it hard for anyone within earshot to resist eavesdropping.

"I dunnoooo," says Shaun Boyle. "I think that may be a wee bit premature. Ammmm… a sheriff on Lundy Island?"

The fisherman says something in response to the conservationist. Diane and Mike subconsciously lean towards him attempting to hear what the fisherman is saying but his utterances are much too soft.

"Sure we sometimes get some eejits here that drink too much and get langers and make some noise," continues Mr. Boyle, "but most people that come over are not dodgy… most people respect the land and the people and the good work we're doing here… we don't need a sheriff I don't think."

Before Diane can ask Mike his opinion on the merits of law enforcement on Lundy Island, their food arrives. Diane's mouth waters at the sight of her beer-battered fish and chips and mushy peas and at Mike's unique sample plate of whelks, crab, sausage, cheese and bread – something not advertised on the menu but mutually concocted by Mike and the chef.

They enjoy their meal thoroughly and neither Diane or Mike are disappointed, even though there is always the chance of disappointment when a restaurant becomes a favourite and expectations are built up so high.

"Lundy Island is truly a special place, isn't it Mike?" says Diane, wiping her mouth after the last bite.

Mike answers with a completely honest smile. This evening together in the tavern goes back to simpler times and allows the two to forget about any worries, from the past or present. They even join in a game of bridge with a pair of locals, even though Mike would normally avoid such interactions with acquaintances. But Diane's social manner is a good influence on the secluded man. The first time he and Diane take their tricks, the retired ops man even finds that he has been enjoying himself.

After finishing their pints and playing who knows how many games of cards, Diane reveals a yawn. It's 11 o'clock and she's not sure if the Puffin's Nest has a curfew. She certainly does not want to disturb Mrs. Poole if she's sleeping.

"I think it's best I turn in for the night," Diane says, disappointed to leave the fun.

"I better be going too," Mike says.

They thank their new friends for the card game and say goodnight to Mr. Wilson, who is still standing behind the bar.

As Mike walks Diane back to the Puffin's Nest, they talk about happy things, like funny shared moments when their families caravanned together, and they ask each other about favourite things, like puddings, films and holidays. They do not talk once about threatening letters, and Diane does not even feel she needs to remind Mike that Inspector Darrell Crothers is arriving on the ferry the next morning. They've already arranged that they'll both be at the pier to welcome the inspector.

After seeing that Diane is safely tucked inside the bed and breakfast, Mike walks back to his yacht with a spring in his step. He decides that tomorrow he'll take his friend sailing to a spot he's never taken her before but thinks she'll adore. It's an area of sea caves and he hopes he'll be able to convince her to snorkel around them. *She's still very adventurous*, he thinks.

Nothing can dissuade Mike's good mood, that is until he tucks into his own bed on the yacht. It's when his eyes shut that his mind starts to wander.

His reverie gradually remembers the sounds of hammers and chisels against concrete, the cheers of people dancing in the streets to pop music being played at full blast...

Although back then, he was never 'off the clock', Mike saw no reason why he could not celebrate too. It was a happy time for he and his team as well. Mike let down his guard and even allowed himself to bop up and down to the music. He remembers looking down to see two children facing one another, and twirling in circles while holding hands.

Mike remembers staring out across the happy crowd, thinking *this is history in the making*. And then a loud *BANG!* pierced through the soundscape.

♠ ♠ ♠ ♠ ♠ ♠

The next morning, Diane is awoken from a sound sleep by the call of a puffin-themed cuckoo clock downstairs. It is just as well because in an hour, Inspector Darrell Crothers should be arriving on the ferry.

Mrs. Poole must be reading Diane's mind, or listening for any sign of movement from her room, because as soon as Diane turns on the tap to splash water on her face she hears a knock.

"Breakfast, Mrs. Dimbleby," pipes Mrs. Poole from the other side of the bedroom door.

Diane, still wiping the sleep from her eyes, rushes out to answer. She opens the door to see the woman balancing two trays, one in each hand. One has fresh-baked scones, a selection of jams, and a fruit bowl on. The other is holding a teapot, teacup and a small carafe of milk.

"I could have come down to get my breakfast," says Diane. "How did you climb the stairs with both those trays? How long have you been awake?"

Mrs. Poole simply laughs, sets the trays down on top of the desk inside the room and scurries back down the stairs.

"Ta, Mrs. Poole," Diane calls after her.

Instead of resuming her 'bird bath', Diane digs into one of the cinnamon scones – while they are still warm – and decides on a blueberry jelly as a complement. She takes a few moments to linger over her hot cup of tea and breakfast, and then returns to the bathroom to get ready for the day.

Downstairs, Mrs. Poole pops out from behind her desk to bid Diane a delightful day. After a little startled jump, Diane wishes Mrs. Poole the same, and goes outside to walk down to the dock.

Diane looks at her watch and realizes there's still 20 minutes before the ferry is due. She slows her pace down to a meander and notices that the bright blue sky is devoid of any clouds. Another gorgeous day – she's been lucky this trip.

For the first time taking this path between the Puffin's Nest and the boat dock, Diane notices what must be one of the letterboxes Mike was telling her about.

I really should try to complete this letterbox trail some time, thinks Diane.

Diane walks up to the letterbox and opens it. Inside she finds a stamp and ink pad. She picks up the stamp and turns it over. When she sees the imprint's shape, she lets out a gasp.

"It's just ink," she says after a moment, to reassure herself.

Ink the colour of blood red is partially covering the stamp; it's shaped like a black crow in flight.

Laughing her silly reaction off, Diane continues down to the wharf. She finds herself on the pier, alone. Mike had told her he would meet her here, but perhaps he is still sleeping. *He is still sleeping.* She decides not to go wake him up. There's no need for them both to welcome Darrell, plus she does not want to miss the inspector's arrival which is due to happen any minute.

It's funny how just the other day, Diane saw Mike waiting for her on the pier… and now she is waving to Darrell coming in on the ferry.

"God bless him," Diane whispers out loud. "He's already good at what he does and he's still got many years to go."

When the ferry is docked, the inspector waits for a family of six (all wearing matching striped shirts) and a couple (who by all accounts appear to be on their honeymoon) to disembark, before joining Diane on the pier. He holds out his hand to shake Diane's, but she ignores the gesture and wraps her arms around his back. She's grown fond of the inspector after the time they've spent 'working cases together'.

"So Mike was going to meet us here too, but he's still asleep," says Diane. "We had a late night last night… well, late for us old fogies… not for you I'm sure!"

"Well, before we go see him, is there anything else you should tell me?" Darrell asks.

While walking the detective towards the marina, Diane repeats the information about the threatening letters and phone calls that Mike has received. She also tells him that the book, although fiction, might make some people in power angry. Finally she tells him that a hard copy of the manuscript has been sent to the publishing house.

Before she can tell the inspector anything further they have arrived at the small port where a half dozen sailboats and a few fishing boats are moored.

"That's his," says Diane, pointing to the tallest, and what appears to be the newest, sailboat of the lot. "That's strange," she adds.

"What's strange?" asks Darrell as they approach Mike's boat.

"All of the hatches are closed… and the windows too."

Diane tells Crothers that it's highly unusual for Mike to shut everything up like that. Normally he leaves at least one or two cabin windows open. He loves the smell of the sea and would feel cooped up otherwise.

"Maybe it was chilly last night," Darrell suggests.

"Or maybe he's taking more precautions," Diane whispers, her voice trailing. What she's thinking is maybe Mike was afraid to have an intruder catch him unawares.

Standing on the jetty in front of Mike's yacht, Diane calls his name. With no answer she calls again, this time louder.

"Maybe he's gone to the…" Diane's voice trails again. There aren't very many places to go to run errands on Lundy Island. Still, it wouldn't be impossible for Mike to forget to meet her and go to The Granite for some breakfast.

Diane climbs aboard with Darrell following behind her. Nothing seems amiss. Mike keeps a clean ship. Diane calls his name again.

Darrell walks around to the cabin entrance and awkwardly knocks on the hatch. Receiving no answer, he opens the hatch door and slowly goes down the steps. With not much sunlight accessing the space, Darrell feels for his torch attached to his belt. He turns it on and shines it slowly around the cabin.

He suddenly stops scanning and zeroes in on a particular spot. He gradually steps towards the focus of his attention, shining the torch resolutely.

"Is there room for me to come down?" asks Diane.

"No! Stay there!" yells Darrell uncharacteristically. "And don't touch anything!"

"Well I say," says a bewildered Diane.

Darrell stops when he's almost touching the edge of the cabin bed. He's never met him, but can only assume that this is Mike Davies lying here. From a distance, one might surmise that this man is sound asleep in his bed, save for one particular detail. And that particular detail is that it appears, at first glance, that his head has been gruesomely bashed in.

With no sign of a snore or a breath, the inspector can only conclude that Mike Davies is not sound asleep, but dead.

Chapter 3

Sergeant Sean Golden can hardly believe it. He prefers to stay standing, and paces back and forth on the ferry as he rides over to Lundy Island. In his years stationed at the Barnstaple police office he's never once been called over to the island for a homicide. He's had to pursue disorderly conduct from drunks and drug abusers, sure, but never a homicide.

Even in the entire County of Devon the murder and homicide rate is low – 15 tops a year – and in North Devon where he is based, there is generally next to none.

And to think, he had been feeling really good about the security of his county. The Devon police force had just organized another successful Firearms Amnesty event. Of course, most of the people who handed in guns were probably not the sort of people that would kill or maim, but turning in their rifles, shotguns and other arms helps prevent any possibility of them falling into the wrong hands.

The 200 arms turned in across Devon would be scrap metal by now – transformed into unrecognizable, unthreatening pieces.

Even some handguns were turned in; not just antique revolvers or pistols from avid historians and collectors, but actual, modern-day handguns. (After the atrocious massacre when Thomas Hamilton murdered 16 children at a primary school in Dunblane, Scotland, the British Parliament effectively banned the possession of handguns.)

That is the beauty of such an amnesty event – no questions asked – so people could hand in banned weapons without fear of repercussion. Sergeant Sean Golden had been honoured to play a part in the initiative of reducing the number of firearms in the County. About 20 guns had been turned into the Barnstaple station – mostly hunting rifles and a BB gun – but this also reassured him that he was living in one of the safest areas of the country… even the world.

Sergeant Golden doesn't know if this particular homicide he's been called to happened from a gunshot or another means. All he was told over the phone – *by an Inspector Crothers, was it?* – was that a homicide happened and the body was at the marina. Perhaps it had not been done on purpose. Maybe a party got out of hand and items were thrown or people were pushed or who knows what…

Sergeant Golden begins to shake ever so slightly. Being 195 cm tall and muscular from his neck down to his ankles – he works out on the weights and a bike he set up right behind his desk at the Barnstaple station – many imagine him to be an insensitive bloke. Yet truth be told, the smallest form of violence, against person or property, touches the heart Golden wears on his sleeve.

The sergeant takes in a deep breath and reminds himself that he's the Island's primary law enforcement contact. He's been called, and he is responding.

♠ ♠ ♠ ♠ ♠ ♠

Diane can hardly believe this has happened. She had not actually believed there was anything really profound to worry about. She had asked Darrell to come to the island only as a precaution - she did not truly think Mike's life was in danger. But now Mike Davies, her lifelong friend, is dead.

"Diane!" Darrell says, a little louder than he'd like. Sitting next to her, he had said her names several times without her responding. Diane is breathing rather quickly, too quickly, and he needs to calm her down before she turns blue.

Diane finally looks up at the inspector who is holding her hand and staring at her with concerned eyes.

"I… I… I think I need to go home, Darrell… can you take me home now?" Diane says.

Darrell does not say anything for some time. He simply puts his arm around her and lets her cry muffled sobs into his chest. They sit there, on the edge of the pier next to Mike's yacht, for several minutes.

Once Diane's sobs subside, Darrell says, "I can walk you back to the Puffin's Nest for a rest if you want. I should stay here at least until the sergeant from the mainland arrives."

"Oh, you should stay for the entire investigation!" says Diane, suddenly snapping out of her state of despair.

"Maybe once you've had a wee bit of a rest, you can help by doing what you do best – using that brain of yours."

"Darrell, we must stay right here – we need to figure out who has killed Mike!" Diane says adamantly, as if it had been Darrell and not her who, just minutes ago, had suggested they leave the island.

Darrell hadn't let Diane go down into the cabin to see the body of her friend, but he had told her that Mike had left this world and not by natural causes.

Diane face becomes resolute, like she's now ready to play the role of investigator rather than grieving chum. Before she stands up to make her way onto the yacht again, Sergeant Sean Golden approaches.

"Inspector Darrell Crothers?" he asks quietly.

"Yes, you must be Sergeant Sean Golden. Thank you for coming so quickly," Darrell says, shaking the Devon County police officer's hand.

The local sergeant is at least a head taller than Darrell and towers over Diane, and yet his height does not give him any edge in the confidence department. Both Darrell and Diane are seasoned when it comes to solving homicides; this would be Sergeant Golden's second homicide case, and the first that he's in charge of.

However, what he's lacking in 'major crimes' experience, he more than makes up for in empathy and gentleness. He places a tender hand on Diane's shoulder, telling her he's sorry for her loss.

"Inspector Crothers told me the victim was a friend of yours," Golden says.

Diane nods and gives the sergeant an appreciative smile.

"Come, Sergeant Golden. I'll take you down to the scene," says Darrell. "Diane, will you be okay waiting here?"

"I'll head back to the Puffin's Nest," says Diane. "Not to sleep but to start working. You can find me there."

Golden tentatively follows Darrell onto the yacht and down the stairs into the cabin. Although he has been expecting to see the corpse, the dead body of Mike Davies still catches him off guard. The amount of blood and the part of his now deformed head nearly makes the sergeant physically ill.

"That's not a gunshot, is it?" asks Golden timidly.

"No. It needs to be confirmed by a medical professional, but it appears to be a blow from an extremely heavy object," says Darrell. "And since an object like that is not close to the body, it's pretty certain it's not an accident."

"Oh, I see… and the body doesn't smell, does it? I thought it would smell, surely, being dead and all," says Golden.

"No, he hasn't been dead long enough," Darrell explains patiently.

"And would this be murder or manslaughter… and if it's manslaughter, would it be involuntary or voluntary…. and if it's involuntary would it be… oh, I'm sorry Inspector Crothers. Of course, we can't know any of that until we find out who's responsible… I'm just a wee bit nervous, that's all."

Darrell tells the sergeant to relax and assures him that he was the same way on his first few murder cases. Darrell tells him that, if he does not mind of course, he would like to handle the case. After all, Mrs. Diane Dimbleby is a close friend of his and the murder victim is a close friend of hers, and since he discovered the body, he has the benefit of probably being the first on the scene since the dirty act was committed. Of course, he would run it by both Golden's superintendent and his own to make sure he has their permission.

"I'd like to see the case through to the end," says Darrell, "but only if you don't mind."

"That's brilliant," says a relieved Golden; then, trying not to sound too excited, he says, "No, I don't mind. I have some other work I should be getting on with anyway."

Darrell smiles. Some police officers can be very possessive of their jurisdiction, but it seems like Golden is most agreeable to share. In fact, he's keen to get out of the immediate vicinity of Mike Davies' body, and does so at a speed much faster than you would expect from such a towering figure.

"Oh, Sergeant Golden," says Darrell, calling after the policeman. "Hold up."

Darrell walks up the steps to the deck of the yacht to see Golden already halfway down the pier. "Golden!" he calls again, which has the intended effect this time.

The sergeant slowly turns around, worried the inspector has changed his mind about taking charge of the case. Heading down, he slowly walks back from whence he came.

"Golden, before you go, can I just ask a favour?" asks Darrell.

"Oh certainly, certainly, please excuse me... I don't know what's gotten into me," says the sergeant.

"Understood," says Darrell. "Can you tell me where the closest GP might be? I need him or her to come and examine the body."

"GP, sir?"

"General practitioner... a doctor... just until I can get my medical examiner, Dr. Jackson, down here. I'll call him at once, but it will still take several hours for him to arrive."

The sergeant tells Darrell that there's actually a retired doctor living on Lundy Island, a Dr. Cartwright. Before Golden goes to fetch him, he lends Darrell his satellite phone – a device he brings with him to the island due to the unreliable mobile service – so the inspector can call Dr. Jackson.

"I knew you had some brain to go along with your brawn," Darrell says with a wink.

Over the phone, Dr. Jackson is not quick to agree to make the lengthy trip to Devon County. After the inspector manages to negotiate adequate compensation – they decided that Darrell would bring the medical examiner a packed lunch every day for a month, and not just a simple sandwich mind you, but a packed lunch that could be described as 'gourmet' – Dr. Jackson agrees to make the trip to Barnstaple to examine the body of Mike Davies formally.

After Darrell resists the temptation to call his wife and children to say, *"I'm calling you on a satellite phone... that means we're being connected by satellites orbiting around space,"* he sees

Sergeant Golden running back towards the marina. An older gentleman, Dr. Cartwright, is hurrying to keep up behind him.

By the looks of some leftover shaving cream on Dr. Cartwright's cheeks, one can surmise that Golden did not give the retired physician much time to ponder the request to come and examine the deceased.

The doctor does not seem to mind. As soon as he introduces himself to Darrell he immediately gets to work. At the top of the yacht's cabin stairs, he asks Golden to hand him his leather Gladstone bag.

"Shall I call about a forensics team, Sir?" Golden asks the inspector.

"Yes, thank you Golden," Darrell says. "I think you're much more suited for this line of inquiry than you think."

As it may be a long wait before forensics can arrive, Darrell joins the doctor in the cabin and takes numerous pictures, using his phone, while Mike Davies is still *in situ*.

The contents of the space reinforce its status as a permanent residence. Photos – some of far-off, tropical places, some of more familiar places, like the Frankfurt Opera House, perhaps – hang on the cabin walls. A stack of books balances next to a lamp on a side table standing next to the bed. A short closet is jam-packed with shirts and trousers hanging from plastic hangers in sporadic order.

Whoever did this knew that Mike essentially lived on this yacht.

"So doctor, can you confirm cause of death?" Darrell asks as Dr. Cartwright replaces his instruments inside his bag.

"Yes, as you suspected, cause of death is most probably a severe blow to the head. This is not my area of expertise, but if I had to wager a reliable guess, I would say he died in the early hours of the morning. I'll note his body temperature for the medical examiner."

"Good, Golden can relay this information to Dr. Jackson when he takes the body to the morgue in Barnstaple," says Darrell. "Thank you Dr. Cartwright for making yourself available at short notice."

Darrell and Dr. Cartwright emerge out of the cabin to see Golden with a slumped posture and looking rather pale… again.

"Are you quite alright?" Dr. Cartwright asks the sergeant, reaching up to feel his forehead.

"I heard the inspector say… you'd like me to accompany the body to the morgue, sir?"

"Why yes, Golden. Now don't you fret. I meant what I said. You have a knack for investigations… detective work. You just need the experience."

Golden's colour returns and he smiles. "I don't have a cadaver pouch, but I bet I could track down a non-porous material quickly – a tarpaulin perhaps – to transport the corpse."

"A non-porous material you say! Well, who's the smart one now?" Darrell cheers. "Might be best to ask one of your mates on the island to help you carry the body over to the mainland… and keep it low profile... you don't want to spook any tourists on the ferry."

"Right!" Golden says, determined.

Golden sets off to locate a non-porous material and someone that has the stomach to help him move a dead body – truth be told, most of the island's residents could probably endure such a deed. Dr. Cartwright volunteers to stay with Mike Davies until the sergeant returns, so Darrell can go and check on Diane at the Puffin's Nest.

After the short climb up the moorland, Mrs. Poole greets the inspector at the bed and breakfast's front door. It's been some time since a male as young and dashing as Darrell Crothers has visited the Puffin's Nest.

"Come through, come through," says Mrs. Poole, a little too keenly. "You must be lost. Come sit and have a cup of tea while we figure out where you're trying to go."

Darrell chuckles. "If this is the Puffin's Nest, I'm exactly where I need to be."

"Oh my," blushes the bed and breakfast's proprietor.

"I'm here to see one of your guests… Mrs. Diane Dimbleby."

Mrs. Poole, slightly disappointed, but remaining as pleasant as always, brings Darrell to Diane's room. She takes the liberty of knocking for the inspector.

"Yes?" Diane says, sounding distracted.

"You have a visitor… a young man… who says he knows you."

"Oh yes, indeed… you can come in Darrell!"

When Darrell opens the door, he sees Diane sitting at her desk intently bent over her laptop. She has been hard at work meticulously reading Mike Davies' manuscript, and not for the first time. In addition to the staff at the publishing house, Diane has also read Mike's novel before. A while back he sent her a digital copy which has been saved on her computer since. She is in the middle of reading one of the more 'hair-raising' passages – one dealing with an intricate strategy used by the MI6 some time ago to extract a fellow agent from an unfriendly territory – when Darrell arrives.

"Do you know much about the Berlin Wall, Darrell?" Diane asks, looking up from her laptop.

"Of course I know there was a wall that divided Germany, but I can't say I know much… why?"

"Well, you would have just been a child or barely a teenager when the Wall came down," says Diane.

Darrell takes a seat, sensing the retired teacher is about to give him a history lesson. He's happy to take a rest for a few minutes. Plus Diane does not normally prattle on, so when she has a lot to say, she normally has an important point to make.

Diane asks Darrell to imagine waking up to find out that a barrier had been created right in the middle of his city – a barrier that nobody is allowed to cross. That means if his friends or relatives or job or favourite place to visit are on the other side, he is not permitted to go to or visit them.

This happened in Berlin, Diane continues. On August 12, 1961, at midnight, East German soldiers and police were commanded to close the border, which crossed through Berlin and divided East and West Germany. Literally neighbours, families and friends were separated. Students could not reach their university to continue their studies. East Germans who had loved ones in a hospital in West Berlin could not go and visit them.

At first the wall was made of barbed wire and blocks, and then it became more fortified and made of cement. Some people successfully snuck over the wall, but others were captured or killed. Diane tells Darrell that one of Mike's colleagues, another British agent, had been trapped in East Berlin, but he did not try to escape while the wall stood.

In 1989, protestors convened next to the Wall which urged the East German government to reopen the border between the East and the West. The gates along the wall were opened. This was the beginning of the fall of the Berlin Wall.

"It was a major celebration – you might remember seeing some of the news coverage on the tele," says Diane. "But something went dreadfully wrong with Mike's colleague."

"So Mike was an MI6 agent?" asks an astonished Darrell

"Yes, and some of his actual experiences with the MI6 are featured in his latest manuscript," Diane explains. "Even though it's a work of fiction, I fear that what he's revealed may have provoked someone to shut him up."

Diane gives the inspector a thumb drive that has a copy of the manuscript on it. She tells Darrell that he should read it as its contents may be essential for solving her friend's murder. That is, if the story is in fact the killer's motive.

Diane also tells Darrell that other than herself, the only people that she knows of who have seen the manuscript are the staff at the publishing house. But with all the latest talk of hacking and spying, one could never be sure how many eyes are lurking about.

"How did you read the manuscript so quickly, Diane? You haven't even been in your room here for an hour. And did you take this thumb drive from the cabin this morning? You know that you shouldn't be taking anything from a crime scene…"

"I've been reading Mike's pages since he began writing the novel," says Diane. "With the publishers' permission, Mike asked me to be his editor on this project. I agreed."

Darrell stares at her blankly for an instant. Then he stands up quickly, practically pouncing towards the closet. He opens it and finds what he's after – Diane's suitcase. He swings it open and lays it on her bed. Forgetting all his manners, he starts grabbing clothes out of the closet and throwing them in the case.

"Darrell!?! What's gotten into you???" an alarmed Diane asks.

A knock comes at the door. "Everything alright in there?" warbles Mrs. Poole from behind the door.

"Yes!" Diane and Darrell yell at the same time.

Darrell listens for the sound of Mrs. Poole's feet going back down the stairs, and then says, "Diane, don't you see? If the killer murdered Mike because of the book, he or she might know that you are the book's editor. And if they know that, you may be next on their hit list. I do not want you anywhere near this place!"

"But—"

"There is no argument you can make that will subtract from the fact that you might not be safe here. I want you on the very next ferry off this island."

But Diane isn't a former MI6 agent. She isn't privy to British Secret Service operations. And it wasn't her that wrote the passages that allude to actual events that some people in power may not want made public. She has just been correcting some basic grammatical errors, the odd typo, and in a few cases has improved phraseology.

Still, she *does* know what happened 25 years ago at the border between East and West Berlin. It was a particular incident Mike wrote about. He thought he had been safe including it in a book of *fiction*. But perhaps he had been wrong.

Diane wonders though, who's to say he wasn't murdered for some completely different reason, like for the classic motives of greed, heartbreak or revenge?

Chapter 4

After it travels through a hallway of doors labelled 'Motive A' through 'Z', Diane's mind returns to the loft on the top floor of the Puffin's Nest Bed and Breakfast. Her eyes focus back on the suitcase that Darrell continues to fill with her very own clothing, which she finds only slightly disturbing. It'd be as if her son or nephew, if she had either, were packing her clothes, and she's nowhere near the state of needing someone to do her packing.

Before Darrell can open the drawer holding her knickers, Diane says, "You said yourself that I could help by doing what I do best – using my brain to help you with this case."

"That was before I knew you were working as the murder victim's editor," says Darrell. "And like *you* said, the book might be the motive."

"That doesn't mean I'm in danger, surely."

"The killer might still be in the area. Don't you think that if he knows that the editor of Mike Davies' book is on the island, he'll want that editor – you – dead!?!"

"Ok, there's no need to blow a fuse," says Diane, feeling deflated in purpose.

She agrees to leave the island as long as Darrell lets her finish her own packing.

Downstairs, Diane informs Mrs. Poole that she is checking out, but that Inspector Darrell Crothers would take over the loft if she has no objections. The inn owner swings her arms in excitement.

She's overjoyed to hear the detective would be staying at none other than the Puffin's Nest.

Diane bends down to pick up the items that Mrs. Poole so boisterously knocked to the floor. She stares down at a letter she's just picked up. It's one that Mrs. Poole had been writing to her sister who lives in County Durham. It isn't so much that the sisters write to one another out of fear that the art of letter writing will become extinct – it's more because neither can stand the other's voice. They much prefer to communicate by post rather than by telephone.

"I'll take that thank you," Mrs. Poole says, swiping the letter from Diane's hands.

"Oh terribly sorry," says Diane. "Thank you, Mrs. Poole, for your hospitality."

Mrs. Poole's letter has stirred up Diane's vault of recent memories. Specifically it has brought her attention to what *had* been an inconspicuous detail, one that the unconscious has collected and has waited for the conscious to catch up. Specifically Diane is remembering the threatening letters that Mike had shown her – the ones that so cruelly addressed him.

When Diane had held the letters in her own hands, while aboard friend's yacht, she must have subconsciously held each of the pages up to the sun. She remembers now seeing a faint image, a watermark. And if it is what she envisions now, the watermark is a familiar one.

She remembers the symbol with wholehearted focus now – a calligraphic *CP*. Diane knows she's seen stationary with that same watermark before, and recently too. The *CP* stands for 'Copse Publishers', the name of the publishing house in Birmingham that Mike has been working with.

The first time Diane read the name, she thought it said 'Corpse Publishers'. Mike naturally corrected her mistake, explaining the name 'Copse' (which means a small wood or thicket of trees) had been chosen to pay tribute to Birmingham's reputation as a city of many trees and parks.

The threatening letters sent to her friend were written on stationary from Copse Publishers. That almost certainly means that someone who works at the publishing house, who has read the manuscript, sent Mike the threats. Did that same person kill him?

Diane stops herself from shouting out what she's just remembered. She shouldn't say such things in front of Mrs. Poole, plus Darrell has enough on his plate right now with supervising the forensic team who will be coming to work the scene on the yacht and coordinating with the Barnstaple morgue to receive Dr. Jackson, so he can conduct the formal autopsy.

At the pier, Diane and Darrell run into Sergeant Golden. He's recruited the conservationist, Shaun Boyle, to help him transport Mike's body to the mainland. The corpse is wrapped in an aqua blue tarp, but ingeniously a long piece of rain gutter is sticking out on either end to make the 'load' resemble some sort of construction material.

Still, as soon as Diane sees the mass wrapped in blue, she knows exactly what, or rather *who*, it is. She becomes weak in the knees and Darrell holds her elbow to keep her from falling. After a couple of long breaths with her eyes closed, Diane regains her composure.

"Inspector Crothers, Mrs. Dimbleby, this is Shaun Doyle," says Sergeant Golden. "He's agreed to help me… you know…."

"This has put the heart crossways in me," says Mr. Doyle. "I just can't believe it. A murder? On Lundy Island!?"

"Shhhhhh!" Diane, Darrell and Sergeant Golden shush simultaneously. Luckily the couple and the single gentleman also waiting for the ferry seem not to have heard.

When the ferry arrives, Darrell gives Diane a hug, something he rarely initiates with his older friend and fellow crime solver. He tells her that he will call her at home to give her an update on how the investigation is going.

Diane follows close behind Sergeant Golden and Mr. Doyle, who manage to carry Mike's body as if they are seasoned construction workers headed to their next job. Diane sits in the row behind them, and several times during the ferry ride finds herself placing her hand on top of the tarp covering her friend's body.

Upon reaching Barnstaple, Diane leaves it up to Sergeant Golden to accompany Mike's corpse to the morgue. She feels relieved to be in the driver's seat of her car again – it seems like it has been ages, even though she's only been away since early yesterday.

The whole drive back to Apple Mews, Diane's mind alternates between thinking about who to notify about her friend's death – as far as she knows, Mike has no living relatives – and Copse Publishers.

In the past, out of all the staff at the publishing house, she's only corresponded with Julie Petrie, the publishing house's executive director, and only by e-mail.

Diane wonders how tight the security is at a publisher's office. It could be possible that someone not even connected to Copse Publishers broke in, read Mike's manuscript and even used some of the publisher's stationary to write the threats. *This would be an intriguing plot line for my next crime novel*, Diane thinks for a brief moment. Her mind quickly shifts to, *how dare I think about my friend's murder in that way right now!*

She suddenly slams on the brakes. The Border Collie in front of her car stops just as quickly. Standing in the middle of the road the dog stares at Diane. If Diane had been lost in thought just a few seconds longer she could have hit the poor dog. The Border Collie stares a moment longer, not with malice in his eyes but concern almost, then finishes crossing the road into an adjacent farmer's field.

"I wish you were here, Rufus!" Diane yells aloud. She is so used to taking her canine companion with her everywhere, but she couldn't have brought him to Lundy Island since sailing was on the books.

Diane continues the drive, more focused this time, and manages to return to Apple Mews without any other mishaps. As soon as she pulls her car into her driveway, she can hear Rufus barking next door. It seems that he is as excited to see her as she him.

Diane runs over to Mrs. Oakley's and knocks, trying not to do so frantically. Mrs. Oakley opens the door, and Rufus bursts out and jumps up to greet his friend and caretaker. Diane wraps her arms around Rufus' shoulders and nuzzles her nose into his fuzzy back.

When she stands up, Diane finally notices the new… 'fur-style' Rufus is donning. The grey terrier's hair that normally hangs naturally over his eyes and nose has been tied into an assortment of buns, each held together with a pink bow.

"Oh my, Rufus, don't you look dashing," Diane giggles.

"I was trying to think of a way to keep his hair clean – it gets in the way when he eats, don't you think?" says Mrs. Oakley. "Perhaps I got a little carried away."

"Nothing wrong with a new style from time to time," Diane laughs again. "Was he a good boy for you while I was away?"

"He was at that, although one time he hid my socks on me, he did! He's a smart one, aren't you Rufus? A little rascal I suspect too."

Mrs. Oakley scratches the terrier behind the ears, sad to see him go. Diane thanks her neighbour for taking care of Rufus and tells her that once she's settled back in, she'll have to invite her over for a nice dinner. What she does not tell Mrs. Oakley is that the invitation may have to wait until the case of Mike Davies' murder is solved.

Diane quickly brings their things inside and then takes Rufus for a walk. Perhaps she is craving the fresh air and exercise as much as or more than the terrier. Diane is feeling spooked to the bone and needs to try and settle her mind.

When their feet touch the village green, Diane unclips the leash, allowing Rufus to run free. Diane follows behind quickly. The power-walker pace is helping her angst morph into calm... that is until, whilst coming around the bend, she smacks into her dear friend Albert.

Diane lets out a squeal, while Albert is more than pleased to see her. Although their relationship is technically platonic, the two retirees are each other's closest companions and confidants. They each envision, in the back of their minds, that they will marry, although the topic has never been broached aloud.

Albert immediately breaks out into a spiel about his latest local history project. "I am not certain... but in or around this very spot, is where the very first recorded game of cricket was played!"

"My stars! The very first game of cricket in the world was right here?!"

"I didn't say that, my dear Diane. But the very first game of cricket in Apple Mews was on this spot... or a spot near this spot."

Diane laughs quite hard until her laughter turns to crying.

"Oh, what is it my dear?" Albert asks, as he passes Diane a handkerchief. "You look like you've seen a ghost."

Albert places an arm around his friend. When Diane catches her breath, she tells him everything: about what's happened to Mike aboard his yacht at Lundy Island, about the threatening letters, about the manuscript and her suspicion that it is the motive.

"You have to promise not to share this with anybody, Albert," Diane says quietly.

"Of course I won't. But what can I do to help?"

"You've already done it," says Diane with a smile. "I feel better having told you. And now I know what I should do next."

Diane wishes Albert luck with his history tour of the game of cricket and reminds him of their upcoming 'mead and mystery' get-together. She whistles for Rufus to come, reattaches his leash, and quickly walks back home.

After filling Rufus' water bowl, Diane turns on her computer and Googles 'Copse Publishers' to look up its phone number. Although it's Sunday afternoon, she's decided to call the executive director anyway. She'll leave a message on Mrs. Petrie's voicemail and that way it will be there waiting for her first thing tomorrow. It's crucial that Diane get a hold of her as soon as possible. And she doesn't want to send the director a message to her work e-mail address, because who knows who will be snooping in the office today.

As she listens to the ringtone, Diane tries to mentally prepare exactly what she'll say on Mrs. Petrie's voicemail. But instead of hearing "You've reached the voicemail of Julie Petrie…," somebody picks up after just two rings.

"Hello, Copse Publishers."

"Um… yes… um… I'd like to speak to Julie Petrie please."

"This is she."

"I didn't expect that you'd be in the office today. I'm sorry if I'm disturbing you. My name is Diane Dimbleby."

"Oh Diane! It's so nice to finally speak to you. I'm such a big fan of your latest book. And you've been doing a smashing job editing Mike's book."

"Mrs. Petrie—"

"Please, call me Julie."

"Julie, I have some terrible news."

Diane tells Julie that Mike Davies is dead. The publisher is stunned. Both women remain quiet for some time until Julie lets out a long sigh.

"I just can't believe he's dead," she says. "Still, if I look at it from a business point of view, this is a blessing in disguise. This being his last book and published posthumously means its sales will surpass all projections!"

Although the publisher's commentary makes Diane cringe slightly, she has to agree. A dead author is like a dead painter – their works are more valuable once they pass away. Nevertheless, this is a murder, and solving it is more important than talking about sales figures.

"I liked the fellow though," says Julie. "He was a bit odd, remote really, but there was something quite endearing about him."

"Julie, there's more," says Diane. She explains that Mike has been killed under very suspicious circumstances, and whatever information Julie has about Mike and his manuscript might be most helpful to Detective Crothers.

"And you say he received the threats after he submitted the final draft to us?" Julie asks.

"Yes," Diane says. She does not tell the publisher that it appears the threatening letters were written on the publisher's stationary. Who knows? Julie Petrie could even be the author of the vile threats.

"Can you make it to Birmingham tomorrow? Why don't you come by my office so we can chat to see if I have anything helpful to offer? Say, 10am?"

"That's fine," says Diane. "I really should bring Detective Crothers with me, being his investigation and all. Is that alright with you?"

"See you both tomorrow morning. Goodnight Diane."

Not only should Darrell be there, but Diane would feel a lot safer with him there too. Knowing what she knows about the watermark on the threatening letters, the publishing house could be a danger zone. Now to somehow make sure the inspector can leave Lundy Island and make it to Birmingham for 10 tomorrow morning.

Diane takes out her wallet and pulls out a folded piece of paper that Sergeant Golden had given her. It has the number of the satellite phone that Golden has generously lent Darrell for the duration of his time on the island. It was mighty smart of Golden to do so and to share the number with Diane. She dials the number, hoping Darrell still has the phone with him.

"Inspector Darrell Crothers."

"Darrell, it's Diane."

"Diane, is everything alright?"

"Oh yes… fine… fine… is there any chance you can be in Birmingham tomorrow at 10 am?"

"Oh Diane… the forensic team has just arrived to finally process the yacht. They might be able to finish by tonight but…"

"I've arranged for us to meet the executive director at Mike's publisher's office."

"Isn't that a little premature?"

"Not if the threatening letters were written on the publisher's stationary."

"Diane!? Why didn't you say anything before?"

"I remembered it later and then when I did you were so busy organizing this and that…"

Diane tells the inspector that the threatening letters should be inside the cabin on the yacht, although she isn't sure where. Darrell pokes his head into the cabin and asks one of the forensic investigators if they came across any typed letters of a threatening nature. The investigator says they haven't, but that they are not finished processing the scene yet.

"The killer could have also taken them," Darrell and Diane say at the same time.

"But the cabin wasn't ransacked, and it didn't even appear to be rummaged through," says Diane.

Darrell then tells Diane that he's already talked to Dr. Jackson about his autopsy on Mike's body. He says a severe blow to the head, probably from a large rock or a similar type of object, was the cause of death. He says Golden and a couple of constables from the mainland are searching the area just to see if they can find a rock with any evidence on it.

"So Golden came back, did he?" Diane says jovially, while trying to ignore Darrell's statements about a 'large rock', 'blood' and ''hair.

"He did!" says Darrell. "I think he's found his footing."

The forensic investigator exits the yacht's cabin and joins the inspector on the pier. In his hands are two worn pieces of paper, each in their own evidence bag.

"Darrell? Are you still there?" Diane asks on the other end of the phone line.

"Just one moment Diane."

"Are these the letters you were after, sir?" the forensic investigator asks.

Darrell takes both in his hands and reads the small font, all caps, typed in the centre of each page. He reads the content to himself:

"DEAR MIKE DAVIES, KINDLY WITHDRAW YOUR LATEST MANUSCRIPT OR ELSE YOUR DAYS ARE NUMBERED."

and

"THIS IS YOUR LAST WARNING. CANCEL THE BOOK DEAL BEFORE IT'S TOO LATE FOR YOU."

He holds the letters up towards the setting sun and can faintly make out a watermark.

"Diane, can you tell me what you remember about the watermark on the threatening letters?"

"I remember a CP in cursive. CP stands for Copse Publishers."

"I'm going to catch the early morning ferry tomorrow and I'll meet you at the publisher's office at 10am."

"Oh, that's wonderful. Thank you Darrell… thank you."

When they hang up the phone, Darrell worries that he may be leaving the island too soon, but the forensic team appears to be almost finished. And Sergeant Golden is turning out to be an excellent second-in-command.

Speaking of Sergeant Golden, Darrell sees him practically sprinting towards him with the constables in tow. The mighty-but-limber police supervisor stops in front of the inspector. He's carrying a heavy object encased in an evidence bag and passes it to Darrell with inquiring eyes.

Darrell carefully handles the large piece of granite and scans it closely. He flips it over and sees a few roughly-ripped strands of white hair stuck to a sharp sliver of the rock – they're held in place by a reddish-brown substance. This could be Mike Davies' hair and blood.

"Well done Golden!" says Darrell, patting the sergeant enthusiastically on the back. "Where did you find it?"

"We searched the entire beach, sir," the Sergeant says, pointing to the rocky shore next to the pier.

"Most impressive!" beams Darrell. "Can I trust you to take this to the lab to test it for fingerprints and DNA?"

"Yes sir!" Golden practically shouts. He cannot hide his full-tooth smile.

Before passing the rock back to Golden, Darrell takes one last look. He wonders how many millions of years old this very piece of granite is and what stories it could tell from across the ages. Was this the very first murder it ever witnessed or played a role in?

Darrell cannot think about that now. He has to concentrate on making sure everything is organized before leaving the island. His biggest challenge perhaps is explaining to Mrs. Poole at the Puffin's Nest that he will not be staying long enough for the full breakfast she promised of poached eggs, griddle cakes, baked beans, grilled tomatoes and 'Old English' sausage.

Chapter 5

Diane finds a spot to park less than a five-minute walk away from Copse Publishers. She leaves the high-traffic road to find the pedestrian-only street where the boutique publisher is located.

The time is five minutes before 10, so most of Birmingham's workforce has already completed their Monday morning commute. Diane finds herself among mostly women, some with tots in tow, window shopping among the procession of independent and name-brand stores.

Diane spots Darrell heading towards a barista holding a tray of samples – some sort of espresso-based drink topped with whip cream – who is outside trying to drum up business for her café. By the looks of the bags under Darrell's eyes he could use several shots of strong espresso.

"You made good time!" Diane says to the inspector, while trying not to laugh at the whiff of whip cream stuck to his nostril. She pulls a napkin out of her purse and points to his nose.

"I got the island's conservationist to run me over to the mainland in his motorboat," says Darrell. "I didn't want to wait until this morning, so as soon as the forensics was done, he took me over last night."

Darrell had taken a brief nap in his car and then drove to Birmingham first thing this morning. Diane shakes her head like a concerned mum. For a moment she wonders whether she should have got her friend involved in this case. But who could do a better job than he?

"Well, we best go meet Mrs. Petrie," says Diane, pointing to the small "Copse Publishers" sign situated above another sign, one that reads "Ainslie Graphic Design." Both signs are bolted above a red doorway, tucked in between a shop selling bath and beauty products and a sushi restaurant.

They climb the stairs to the second floor to the publishing house. Darrell is a little surprised by the size of the office. As far as he can tell the entire space is three rooms at best; two offices and one reception room. It's definitely not as large as he expected it to be.

"Well, they are not a magazine or a newspaper publisher, pushing out a new issue every day or every month" whispers Diane. "They publish books, and only a few a year. And the actual printing happens in London."

"Newspapers? Do they still exist?" Darrell whispers with a smirk.

He then realizes it works to their advantage that Copse Publishers is smaller than he had anticipated. This means dealing with less potential "persons of interest"… it means the pool of people who had been technically allowed to read Mike Davies' manuscript is small.

Darrell suddenly realizes that he forgot to ask Dianne whether she told Mrs. Petrie about the threatening letters and how they were written on Copse Publishers' stationary.

As if she is reading the inspector's mind, Diane quickly whispers, "I did not tell her about the watermark on the pages of the threats."

She's told Darrell just in time as they hear footsteps from the back office coming out to meet them.

A short and spry woman dressed in a black pantsuit and pumps has come out to meet them. The skin tone facial concealer and her freshly-dyed, bright red hair do well to hide the marks she's developed over the 30 years she's spent working long hours in the publishing business.

"I'm Julie Petrie," she says, firmly shaking Diane's hand. "Diane, it's so nice to finally meet you face to face, even though the circumstances are not... the most comfortable."

She then introduces herself to the inspector. As she firmly shakes Darrell's hand too, he looks her straight in the eyes. The publisher does not flinch one bit.

"Thank you for taking the time to meet with us," says Darrell. "Is there somewhere we can sit and chat?"

Mrs. Petrie nods her head. She runs back to get her purse and invites Diane and the inspector to join her for a coffee at the café a few doors down. Once outside she tells them that it is perhaps better they speak outside the office.

"Since talking to you yesterday, Diane, it got me thinking," Mrs. Petrie whispers. "The walls might have ears, as they say."

Before Darrell or Diane can ask her if she suspects someone from the office in particular,

Julie Petrie turns around and briskly walks towards the Java & Vanilla Bean Café. She swings open the purple-painted door that is bordered with painted images of multi-coloured mugs with steam rising above. Darrell jogs up to catch the door that Mrs. Petrie is holding open.

A young woman with dreadlocks tied into a bun and a sedate but genuine smile asks them if they would like anything to eat or drink. Julie orders a 'non-fat, extra-foam, extra-hot cappuccino in a large mug'; Diane and Darrell each order a cup of tea.

There are no customers in the café. They sit down at a small table, the one furthest from the counter. Diane and Darrell each take out a small notebook. They look at each other and nod their heads – it can't hurt for both of them to write down some pertinent details.

For a moment, Julie plays with the poetry magnets attached to a metal clipboard that is dangling just above their table; she then decides she'd better get on with it. She pulls her mobile out of her pocket and holds up the screen so only Darrell and Diane can see. She slowly swipes to show them pictures of four individuals, three women and one man. Each of them, knowingly posing for the camera, is clearly in an office environment at the time the pictures are taken. They are either sitting at a desk or beside a bookcase or a photocopier.

"Are these all of the employees who work for Copse Publishers?" Diane asks.

"Yes," says Julie. "And these are the people – the only people – who have read the hard copy of the manuscript."

"To your knowledge…" says Darrell, who stops short when the barista delivers their hot drinks to the table. When she leaves, Darrell asks, "Is it possible that anyone else has been in the office and accessed it?"

"I've been keeping the soft copy only on a flash drive, which I locked in the safe along with the hard copy," says Julie. "I checked again this morning and both are still locked up tight."

Julie explains that she asked each of her employees to read the hard copy and to give her their notes. As each borrowed the pages, she had them sign them out to make sure the manuscript was always accounted for.

"Is it possible that any one of them took the manuscript out to read at a restaurant or another public place during their lunch hour?" asks Diane.

"Oh it's possible, yes, but I would hope they wouldn't be daft enough to leave the pages out on a table, unsupervised. Oh God, I hope not," says Julie. "But the reason I brought you here, away from the office, is I have to tell you about one of my employees."

Julie holds up her phone and swipes back to the picture of Ingrid Bauer, who works as a copy editor but also does some online marketing for the small publishing house. Diane stares at the picture to see a woman, smiling yes, but with eyes that are not reciprocating.

Ingrid Bauer had told Julie that she tragically lost her father 25 years ago, right around the time of the fall of the Berlin Wall. Her father had been an East German soldier and had been in charge of guarding a British agent, an agent who had been captured on the East Berlin side of the Wall. The British agent was part of MI6. He then was successfully rescued, but during the extraction Ingrid's father was apparently killed.

"Ingrid said, 'The MI6 shot and killed my father. The MI6 are murderers!' She was quite emotional…understandably," recounts Julie.

"When did she tell you all of this?" asks Diane.

"Right after she read the manuscript," says Julie.

Diane and Darrell look at one another without saying a word. The inspector hates to jump to conclusions, but it looks like Ingrid Bauer has made it to the top of the suspect list. He will need to interview her as soon as possible. As for the other three individuals in Julie's photographs – the other Copse Publishers employees – they do not appear to have any particular personal interest in Mike Davies' story. But as we all know, appearances can be very deceiving, and Darrell should interview all of the publishing house personnel, including a formal interview with Julie Petrie. But first he has to make an appearance at the station in Shrewsbury. He is due to see the superintendent this afternoon.

Diane and Darrell thank Julie for meeting with them and leave her to finish her especially foamy cappuccino.

"Diane, do you mind walking me to my car?" Darrell asks, as they leave the Java & Vanilla Bean.

Diane looks around at the casual pedestrians and shopkeepers in a jocular fashion. "Are you wanting me to protect you from this suspicious crowd?" she says in jest.

"Hardy har har… I just want to run something by you," says the detective.

Darrell opens the boot of his Range Rover and climbs in. Diane stares after him, amused, wondering what he's up to. Then she sees a small safe pushed against the back seat and Darrell is punching in the security code to open it.

"You can never be too careful…" says Diane.

"Ever since my wife's car was broken into last year, I thought I better get a safe. All the robbers took was some footie equipment, but I kept thinking what if it had been my car and they had gotten their hands on some police evidence… or my lucky fishing lures," Darrell winks.

The inspector passes Diane some pages held in evidence bags. She's seen these before, and not too long ago: "DEAR MIKE DAVIES, KINDLY WITHDRAW YOUR LATEST MANUSCRIPT OR ELSE YOUR DAYS ARE NUMBERED" and "THIS IS YOUR LAST WARNING. CANCEL THE BOOK DEAL BEFORE IT'S TOO LATE FOR YOU."

"Can you confirm with one hundred percent certainty that these are typed on Copse Publishers' stationary?" Darrell asks.

"If you had asked me this morning at quarter to 10, I would have said yes, but with 95 percent certainty. You see, I think I must have recycled the hard copy letters Julie Petrie had sent me using her company's stationary. They were basically generic monthly newsletters sent out to a mailing list. Our main correspondence, Julie's and mine, specifically about Mike's book, had been through e-mail," Diane says. "But now I can say with absolute certainty that these letters have the Copse Publishers' watermark."

Diane pulls out a folded piece of paper from her pocket. She unfolds it and holds it next to the letters encased in the evidence bags. Just to be sure she holds all of them up to the sun to reveal the cursive *CP* symbols at the bottom of each page.

"I nicked the page from a pile on the front desk when Julie ran to get her purse," beams Diane.

"You little devil!" Darrell laughs. "I'll be in touch soon. Try to get some rest, will ya?"

Diane leaves the inspector so he can get on his way to Shrewsbury. Before heading back to Apple Mews, she decides to walk back to the Java & Vanilla Bean – she'd quite like to try one of those foamy cappuccinos herself.

Whilst thinking about Ingrid Bauer, Diane almost walks right into a mom pushing a double pram with a baby and tot inside; and again almost into a greyhound and his owner. But Diane cannot help thinking about the section of Mike's book that must have entirely floored Ingrid.

How Mike described the rescue of the MI6 agent was so vivid, and it did include an East German soldier being fatally shot. The level of detail, the emotion his phrases carried, made Diane feel that this had actually happened, and that Mike had not only witnessed the course of events, but had also been deeply affected by them. Diane had not dared ask him how accurate the depiction was nor did she inquire about what role he played. She was positive Mike hadn't been the captive, but perhaps he had been part of the team that rescued the agent. Maybe Ingrid Bauer thought so too – maybe she even thought Mike Davies had been the one that pulled the trigger and killed her father.

Passing by the window of the café, Diane sees that Julie is no longer sitting at the round table far from the counter. She re-enters the purple door and joins the queue inside the now busier Java & Vanilla Bean.

After pulling out her wallet, Diane looks to the front of the line and sees a slender woman, perhaps 40 years of age, with slightly dishevelled, sandy blond hair. Diane swears she looks similar to one of the photos she'd just seen on Julie's mobile phone.

"Are you having a dark roast today, Ingrid?" asks the barista with the dreadlocked hair.

Diane drops her wallet on the floor. Her clumsiness due to being caught off guard has made a noise so loud that everyone in the café, including Ingrid, looks her way. Diane quickly picks the wallet up, looks in Ingrid's eyes for a brief moment, and scurries out of the café.

"I think I'll have a cuppa when I get home," Diane says under her breath, and she hurries towards her car.

♠ ♠ ♠ ♠ ♠

When Darrell arrives at the Shrewsbury Police Station, he finds the superintendent sitting at Darrell's desk.

Darrell has great respect for Superintendent Ian Groves, a superior who can be stern when he needed to be, but who is always fair. When he sees Darrell, he shoots him a warm but serious smile.

"You've covered a lot of territory the last couple days, Crothers," says the superintendent in his husky voice.

"Yes, sir."

"As you know, I have no objection to the work you're doing – we haven't had much to worry about around here lately, so I like to share resources when we can."

"Thank you, sir."

The superintendent tells him that there is someone here who wants to talk to "Inspector Crothers" especially. All that he's told Superintendent Groves is that he's Agent Somerset from MI6.

"I can't say I'm surprised, based on what you've told me about your murder victim's work history," says the superintendent.

Darrell can't help but smile. The grapevine, in instances such as these, works faster than emails or text messages. Still, is it a tad disconcerting that an agency like the MI6 would still be keeping such active tabs on their retired agents?

The superintendent leads Darrell into his office and shuts the door. Agent Somerset stands when they come in.

"Agent Somerset, this is Inspector Crothers."

The two men shake hands but neither sits. The superintendent walks around the desk to sit in his own chair, and with a determined look, urges Darrell to do the same. The agent follows suit but only after he begins to talk.

"I am aware of Mike Davies' sudden death, and I'm sure you have already uncovered that he was a retired MI6 agent," he says.

The superintendent and Darrell nod, and Darrell says, "May I ask how you came to know about his death... and this inquiry?"

Agent Somerset ignores Darrell's question and says, "It is probably some vandals living on or around the island who are responsible."

"With all due respect," says Darrell, "the evidence we've retrieved so far doesn't really point to the work of vandals. We have to explore all motives and all possible suspects."

"May I remind you that Lundy Island does not fall under your jurisdiction," says Agent Somerset. "And in the grand scheme, the Shrewsbury Police rank low within Britain's chain of command."

"Are you trying to scare me? Stop me from investigating this murder?"

"I'm trying to do what's best for Great Britain," says the agent in a pretentious tone. "And let me make myself clear, the British government does not want something from twenty-five years ago to come out of the shadows to be scrutinized."

Before Darrell can say another word, Superintendent Groves quickly stands and thanks the agent for coming in. "Duly noted," the superintendent says, shaking Agent Somerset's hand.

Darrell knows that the superintendent and he have to bow to the powers-that-be, but he can't help thinking the MI6 has just a little too much power in this instance. A murderer will go free if he is not able to proceed with this investigation, and why? Is it because the MI6 is afraid of looking bad? Or is there more to it than that?

When Superintendent Groves returns from seeing the agent out, he shuts the door anticipating a loud reaction from Darrell.

"In all my 15 years as a detective, I have never been asked to *not* investigate any crime, let alone a homicide!" Darrell yells.

He tells the superintendent about how the threatening letters that Mike received were typed on Copse Publishers' stationary, and how an employee at the publisher's office, Ingrid Bauer, is a viable suspect. The fact that a scene in the book strongly mirrors what actually happened to her father could very well have incited her to commit a murder. And now because the MI6 wants to cover up an old story, she is to remain free?

"Do you think that this Ingrid Bauer thought Mike Davies made light of what happened twenty-five years ago and that angered her?" asks Superintendent Groves. "Or do you think this angered someone in the MI6?"

The two men sit and ponder this for a while. Was it that Mike made light of that event or did he share too many details about what happened? One thing is for sure – if his book is the motive of his murder, he certainly paid for writing about that time in history with his life.

"I need to at least interview Ingrid Bauer, sir?"

"I'm inclined to agree with you Darrell," says the superintendent. "I don't like the idea of a murderer going free either, just because the MI6 decides they don't want their skeletons to fall out of the closet."

Superintendent Groves tells Darrell that he will talk to his own superiors immediately and get to the bottom of this – to find out whom, from on high, is calling the shots about the murder investigation of Mike Davies.

Chapter 6

Upset and frustrated from his meeting with Agent Somerset, Darrell needs to blow off some steam. Although for a brief moment he is tempted to blow off everything and go far away to some fishing cabin in Scotland, or even Canada for that matter, he quickly decides he is not going to give up. MI6 or no MI6, Mike Davies deserves justice.

Darrell calls his wife Claire to tell her he's going to visit Diane Dimbleby before going home. Claire can sense the strain in her husband's voice and she's grateful he's found someone he can talk to when times get tough, as she knows a role in law enforcement often does get challenging emotionally, not that Darrell would ever admit this. Before his mum had passed away she had been a great comfort to her son. It seems Darrell has a similar bond with Diane, except that she also seems to like to get quite involved with investigating murders – something Darrell's mum did not like so much.

When Darrell arrives at Diane's Apple Mews home, she, as always, is not surprised. She's made an extra large pot of tikka masala, and anticipating the inspector might stop by, she's added more chicken than she might normally – she usually adds as many or more carrots and beans as chicken to the mix.

"You're just in time to have some chicken and veg masala," says Diane, opening the door.

"I'm sorry for not calling first," Darrell says almost meekly.

"No need to call first, my friend," says Diane. "If you don't mind me saying so, you look as if you've just been in a boxing match, although there is no clear sign of who won."

"Well, you're not far off," says Darrell, managing to crack a small smile.

Sitting down at the table, while they tuck into the deliciously spicy dish, Rufus does a good job of calming Darrell down and even cheering him up. The dog cannot seem to get enough of the inspector's attention. Rufus has quickly realized that he loves to lie across Darrell's feet. When his deep breaths become louder and louder snores, Darrell for a time forgets about how angry and frustrated he is, and bursts into laughter.

"I think you make Rufus very comfortable… literally and figuratively," smiles Diane.

When Darrell's laughter subsides, he tells Diane about the meeting he had with his superintendent and the MI6 agent, Agent Somerset.

"He basically had the gall to tell me not to carry on with the investigation. He said the British government does not want events from twenty-five years ago to be public knowledge…"

"Has Agent Somerset read Mike's book?" Diane asks.

The question catches Darrell off guard; he hadn't thought of that. He has no idea whether the agent would have read the manuscript, but how could he of? Well, he is a spy so he must have his ways…

It would make sense that Agent Somerset read the manuscript, since he was hinting about not wanting the events that happened twenty-five years ago in Berlin – events that inspired Mike's novel – to come to light.

"Do you think he did?" asks Darrell.

"Well, if this Agent Somerset knows about the book and its contents, he could have been the one who decided to eliminate Mike, with the MI6's blessing of course," Diane says.

Darrell shudders. Would the MI6 actually kill one of their own? Still, he agrees that it is an avenue worth exploring. Being in a room with Agent Somerset again could potentially make the inspector's blood boil. Darrell would have to make sure to mentally prepare for that interview, so he wouldn't let his anger flare up again, although it rarely did.

"Well, if Somerset or any of his fellow agents had something to do with Mike's death, it makes sense that he told me that the highest authorities do not approve of me investigating," says Darrell. "It's the perfect cover. For all we know, his superiors might not even know about Mike Davies."

Diane suddenly has a flashback to a time before Mike had even joined the MI6.

"He must have been barely 18," Diane tells Darrell. "My family was visiting with his in London. Mike had joined the army and was going off to the academy for training in a few days. His mother made him try on his uniform for us. When he came out in his camouflage and cap, I remember he was blushing. He wasn't ashamed I don't think, just unsure. It was always expected he would join up just like his dad. He was perfectly capable – both athletic and intelligent. I do remember him admitting to me though that he was scared. Of course he did fine, so fine that he was a top choice when the MI6 was recruiting."

Darrell's mobile phone rings. He apologizes to Diane, but he has to pick it up – it's his superintendent calling. Superintendent Groves says he's sending a female officer to spend the night at Diane's home. He's just got off the phone with a friend in London who knows a little more about the ins-and-outs of government agencies.

"Your friend is in serious danger," says the superintendent.

"Diane? Are you sure? Why?" Darrell asks.

"Well, let's just say the MI6 might stop at nothing to eliminate any possible *witness*, someone privy to an event that might make the agency vulnerable… an event like in Germany, twenty-five years ago," says the superintendent. "They do not want to compromise their security… their secrecy… their integrity."

Darrell is beyond surprised that Diane has been identified by the superintendent's 'intel' as a serious target. Sure, Darrell himself had been worried about her when they were on Lundy Island, so close to where the murder happened. But surely her life isn't at risk while she's in her very own Apple Mews… at least her life shouldn't be at risk *again*. Like they say, "lightning never strikes the same place twice" – or is that just a myth?

"Do you really think MI6 would kill an innocent civilian, superintendent?" asks Darrell "I mean it's plain barmy! And besides, wouldn't the five people who work at Copse Publishers also be on their… kill list… too?"

"I know it sounds ludicrous," says Superintendent Groves. "But until I speak to the top brass in London tomorrow morning, and find out who is in charge and who is actually a threat, I want to make sure Mrs. Dimbleby is safe. Besides, her life has been threatened more than once during… *ahem…* several other murder investigations."

The superintendent is right. How can Darrell even question the presence of an officer keeping an eye on Diane? He vividly remembers the time she was kidnapped and could have been easily killed, and the time that dreadful Mrs. Rosalyn Thomas and her son broke into her house to take her down. It's amazing that this brave woman is still willing to be Darrell's confidant and fellow sleuth.

They hear a knock at the door.

"That'll be the officer that's coming to stay the night," says Darrell, opening the door. "Hello Shannon, thank you for coming."

Darrell introduces Diane to Constable Shannon Toft. While Diane does not feel she needs the extra attention, she's happy for the company. The inspector takes his leave and Diane puts on the kettle so the two women can share a cuppa before Diane and Rufus head up to bed.

While Diane sleeps soundly for the first time since Mike Davies was killed, Darrell does not sleep a wink. But he hasn't been tossing and turning in bed next to his wife – the inspector has intentionally stayed awake.

After leaving Diane's place the night before, Darrell headed to Birmingham. More specifically, he drove to a street with a series of three to five-storey apartment buildings. Inside one of these buildings is the flat that Ingrid Bauer calls home. Darrell is parked across the street from said building and has successfully managed to stay awake. It hadn't been an easy task, since the cumulative lack of sleep has been catching up with him. To keep from dozing off he consciously tried to think of highlights of his children's lives from every year they've been alive.

Darrell had no problem thinking of examples – their first steps, holidays and fishing excursions, Chloe scoring her first goal, Jeremy winning an art contest – but it had been a little difficult to figure out how old they were when certain events happened. He had to stop himself from calling Claire a couple times to say, "Do you remember when…." He's sure she would have liked to share these memories with him – just not at three o'clock in the morning.

But now it's just a few minutes after six and the first sunrays are shining through his Range Rover's windshield. Darrell is starting to wonder if he's wasting his time. It's probable that like most people, Ingrid Bauer sleeps at night. Why did he think he'd catch her sneaking away from her apartment in the middle of the night? And for what reason? If she had killed Mike Davies, there isn't anything for her to clean up in Birmingham... or is there?

Still Darrell decides he'll stay until 8:30 or 9, when Ingrid might be more likely to head out, possibly even to the publisher's office.

Darrell's determination is slightly rewarded. To his sheer luck, he sees a man unlock the little news stall that's on the pavement just a few metres away. By the looks of a poster on the side of the stall, it looks the small business not only sells newspapers and magazines, but also coffee and tea. Darrell would even settle for a lukewarm beverage at this point.

He gives the owner a few minutes to get settled before heading over to see if he's able to purchase a small bit of comfort in a Styrofoam cup, all the while keeping an eye on Ingrid Bauer's building's main entrance.

"I don't suppose you have any coffee brewing?" Darrell asks.

"I do," says the short, thick side-burned man, who looks to be around Darrell's age. "By the looks of it, you could use a whole pot!"

"How about we start with a cup," Darrell laughs.

"I saw you in your car when I got here. Were you waiting for me to open? I didn't think my coffee was that good," the gentleman laughs.

"Truth be told, I'm doing some surveillance," a tired Darrell says somewhat recklessly.

"Not on me, I hope," the stall owner laughs.

"No," laughs Darrell. "But just to warn you, I'll be here for a few more hours."

"I'll keep the coffee coming then," the man smiles.

"Ta," says Darrell, pouring more sugar and cream into his cup than usual.

Sitting in the driver's seat and devouring the hot newsstand coffee, Darrell gets a second wind, or perhaps a third or a fourth. He's staring intently at the people in business suits and casual dress, and the mums or dads with their kids in school uniforms, rushing out the door of Ingrid Bauer's building. He quickly looks at his watch to realize it's already a few minutes after 8 am. Just as Darrell takes out his mobile, about to ring Claire to see how she and the kids are getting on, somebody knocks on the passenger door window. It's the newsstand owner – bless him, he's carrying another cup of coffee. Darrell lowers the window.

"This is on the house," says the newsstand man. "It's not every day I can show my appreciation to a copper!"

"Ta," smiles Darrell.

"There's something I've been wondering if I should tell ya," says the man.

"Go on," says Darrell.

He tells the inspector about how yesterday, a car had been parked in the very spot where Darrell is now, for several hours. He remembers it well because it was a BMW Series 4 Gran Coupé, and cars like that seldom make an appearance in this neighbourhood. The windows were tinted, and since he thought no one was in the car, the newsstand man took a couple pictures with his phone – he was going to show them to his son, who loves cars.

"Well, as soon I started taking pictures, someone got out of the car and started yelling at me."

"What did he look like?" asks Darrell.

"He was tall, about your height, brown hair… he had on a suit and some sunglasses. After I told him I was just going to show the photos to my son, he still made me delete them. He then got back in the car and stayed for another hour…"

"Thank you for telling me," says Darrell.

There could be a thousand explanations as to who the man in the BMW was and what he was doing parked here for so long. For all Darrell knows, the mystery man could have been pulled over to have a lengthy chat on his mobile with his mum. But is there a possibility it could have been MI6?

Just as the inspector starts to wonder again whether he's wasting his time, just sitting here waiting for perhaps *nothing* that will help solve the case, his mobile starts to ring. It's his superintendent calling.

Darrell picks up and learns the most unexpected… the most startling… the most eerie news – eerie because he's so physically close to the person and place for which the superintendent is calling about. Superintendent Groves has just said, "Ingrid Bauer is dead."

A neighbour had found her body. Apparently, the neighbour heard Ingrid's cat meowing, which wasn't out of the ordinary except that this morning it had been so loud that it caused the neighbour to be concerned. She opened Ingrid's front door – which by chance happened to be unlocked – after knocking for several minutes. It doesn't necessarily matter how or why the neighbour found Ingrid dead, unless Ingrid died by foul play, and if that was the case, the neighbour's story would have to be questioned and analysed.

But Darrell isn't thinking about all of this... yet. He takes in a deep breath and, for some reason, his first thought is that the MI6 definitely has something to hide.

Superintendent Groves tells Darrell that police have been dispatched to the scene. Darrell decides he better wait for them to arrive before going into the apartment himself.

When the Birmingham police cruiser arrives, Darrell walks over and introduces himself to the constables. He briefly explains that Ingrid Bauer, the person who is presumably dead, is involved in a case he is currently working on. The officers voice no objection and in fact take the senior officer's lead in approaching the apartment.

They walk into the lobby, and Darrell and the constables show the concierge their ID. Darrell tells him they've been called to investigate Ingrid Bauer's apartment and the concierge obligingly takes them up in the elevator to the third floor. The concierge is all set to let them into her flat, except they find that her front door is already wide open.

"Thank you for taking us up here," says Darrell to the concierge. "We'll take it from here."

The concierge hesitantly returns to the elevator, while Darrell and the constables slowly walk inside the flat. In the room closest to the door, they see a young woman, clearly in shock, sitting in a chair next to a body lying on the floor. The young woman is almost certainly the neighbour, and the body is almost certainly Ingrid Bauer. Although Darrell has thought about Ingrid Bauer almost constantly for the last 24 hours, he suddenly realizes that he has never actually met the woman in the flesh.

Now he's staring down at her – someone still too young to have left this world – and clearly sees the bullet wound in her head and the gun lying next to her side. Without saying a word, the woman in shock stands and passes Darrell a piece of paper.

Before he even reads the words on the page, Darrell finds himself looking for any distinctive watermark on the piece of paper, but does not find any. In typewritten font, the note reads,

"NOW THAT MY FATHER'S KILLER IS ELIMINATED, I'VE NOTHING ELSE TO LIVE FOR.
SINCERELY, INGRID BAUER"

This sounds like a suicide note and a confession all in one.

Darrell notices in the corner of the room, a desk with both a laptop and a printer – this could have been where the letter was produced.

'*Now that my father's killer is eliminated...*' This must mean that Ingrid believed Mike Davies had killed her father (*had Mike killed her father?*).

So she must have avenged her father's death… but in the letter she does not necessarily admit that she killed Mike Davies, did she?

Darrell slowly walks over to the desk. Ingrid's computer has gone to sleep but the printer is still turned on. He puts on a pair of gloves and presses a random key on the keyboard. The laptop screen comes to life to reveal an open word processing document. The text cursor is blinking next to the end of the typed note, next to the words 'SINCERELY, INGRID BAUER.'

Darrell opens the top drawer of the desk and spots a notebook. He picks up the notebook and flips to the last handwritten entry. Skimming the previous entries, common phrases jump out: *'The British government is to blame'* and *'the MI6 killed my father'*…

When she hears the phone ringing, Diane quickly runs inside from the backyard, where she and Constable Shannon Toft are playing catch with Rufus.

"Hello?!"

"Diane, quick, turn on BBC Radio 4!" shouts Albert over the phone.

Diane knows her friend and if he is taking the time to call her to tell her to listen to something on the radio, there must be a good reason. Without hanging up, she runs over to the radio that is sitting on the kitchen counter – it's already tuned to BBC Radio 4.

"ACCORDING TO A PRESS RELEASE PROVIDED BY JULIE PETRIE OF COPSE PUBLISHERS, THE FICTION BOOK THAT HER COMPANY WILL PUBLISH NEXT MONTH IS INSPIRED BY MIKE DAVIES' TIME WITH THE SECRET INTELLIGENCE SERVICE. PETRIE SUGGESTS THAT THE DEATH OF DAVIES MAY BE CONNECTED TO HIS BOOK; SHE ALSO STATES THAT INGRID BAUER, DECEASED, WHOSE BODY WAS FOUND THIS MORNING, ALSO HAD A CONNECTION TO DETAILS IN DAVIES' STORY. POLICE HAVE NOT YET REVEALED THE CAUSE OF BAUER'S DEATH, ALTHOUGH A WITNESS, WHO HAS ASKED NOT TO BE NAMED, SAYS BAUER TOOK HER OWN LIFE... IN OTHER NEWS..."

"Oh my goodness! Ingrid Bauer is dead!?" Diane gasps.

"So it *is* your friend Mike they are talking about then?" Albert asks with an empathetic tone.

"Yes... thank you for calling Albert. I had no idea of this latest development."

"Diane, are you quite alright?"

"I've had a constable here with me overnight, so I'm being protected, but I don't think I'm in the line of fire," Diane says, mustering a little laugh.

"See you tomorrow?"

"Yes, tomorrow Albert, although I haven't gotten much writing done to share with you," says Diane.

"My dear, you and you alone are more than enough to make an old man like me happy," Albert chuckles.

When the two friends hang up, Diane calls Rufus in for his supper. Constable Toft follows the dog inside. Her smile quickly morphs into a look of concern when she sees Diane's overwhelmed expression.

Before the constable has time to ask Diane what's wrong, there's a knock at the door. Diane starts to go towards it, but is quickly stopped by Constable Toft who insists on answering it instead.

To both Diane and Constable Toft's relief, it is Inspector Darrell Crothers standing on the other side of the front door. He thanks the constable for pulling the overtime and sends her home, but not before Diane insists the officer take home some muffins just baked that morning.

When Diane and Darrell are each settled on the couch with a glass of wine in hand, she tells him about what she heard on the radio.

"I heard the same story on another station while driving here," says Darrell. "And the superintendent says it's on the tele too. By nightfall, all of the UK will be aware of Mike Davies and Ingrid Bauer and MI6's cover-up."

"Julie Petrie really wants to milk these tragedies as much as she can all in the name of book sales, although I'm proud of my friend, Mike, and his book," says Diane. "But I still can't believe

Julie Petrie went to the press so quickly after Ingrid Bauer took her own life."

"If she did take her own life," says Darrell quietly.

"You don't think it's a suicide?"

Darrell says that they still do not have the full medical examiner's report, and he isn't completely convinced that MI6 might not have something to do with her death. The suicide note had been typed, and it was not even signed, so anyone could have written it. Plus he had seen several people go in and out of Ingrid Bauer's building throughout the night. While none of them stood out, who knows if one of them shot Ingrid?

"The one advantage of Julie Petrie going public," Darrell says, "is that your life is no longer in danger. What Mike wrote about, about his and MI6's time during the fall of the Berlin Wall, is no longer a secret."

Darrell's mobile rings. He looks and sees that it is Dr. Jackson who is calling. He, *again*, through more coaxing and promises of breakfasts along with packed lunches, had convinced the medical examiner to do one 'last' favour and go to Birmingham to examine the body of Ingrid Bauer. Dr. Jackson says he isn't finished with the examination yet, but wanted to let Darrell know that no gunshot residue was found on Ingrid's hands.

As the doctor explains though, this does not rule out suicide. Apparently, those who fire a gun do not necessarily test positive for GSR in one hundred percent of cases. And unfortunately, Dr. Jackson discovered that before he arrived in Birmingham, fingernail scrapings were mistakenly taken before GSR samples were gathered. This means if Ingrid Bauer did have gunshot residue on her hands, it could have been wiped away.

When he hangs up the phone with the medical examiner, Darrell tells Diane the latest development.

"So let's imagine Ingrid Bauer did not kill herself... do we then think MI6 did?" Diane posits.

"At least a part of me imagines they could be responsible," says Darrell.

"Did you ever find any evidence on the rock that was found at Lundy, the possible murder weapon that killed Mike?" asks Diane.

"We confirmed the hair and blood to be Mike's, but we found no fingerprints and no DNA belonging to anybody else," Darrell explains.

"So who had a greater motive to kill Mike? Ingrid with her anger, or the MI6 and their need for discretion?" says Diane.

"We might never know," says Darrell.

Diane changes the subject and tells Darrell her plans on how to pay tribute to her friend. She has already started working on a eulogy to read at his funeral. She wants to remind everyone of his loyalty and his desire for transparency and justice for all.

Since Mike had requested that he be cremated when he died, Diane came up with an idea. She is going to arrange for some of their mutual friends to take a bit of his ashes with them on their travels.

His dream had been to sail around the world on his yacht, so at least this way he would still get to cover a lot of distance and be brought to various parts of the world.

"We should say a toast for your friend," says Darrell, raising his glass.

Diane smiles and says, "Keep them straight, Mike!"

He may have risked his life writing this last book, Diane thinks, but he did it because he really did believe in justice for all.

In Mauerpark in Berlin, a young teen is juggling a football masterfully with his feet. Fully focused on the ball, he rams right into someone and falls to the ground. Disoriented for just a moment, the boy reopens his eyes to see the person who he must have collided into already a number of strides away. He watches after the person who is clothed in a dark hood and long coat. The teen stands up and finds himself following behind at a safe distance. He's not sure why he's following, but feels compelled to do so.

After about five minutes of walking, the teen sees the person stop and stand very still next to a remaining piece of the former Berlin Wall. The person kneels and slowly puts something down on the ground. After a long pause, the person continues on his or her way.

The teen, now very curious, quickly walks to the spot next to the graffitied section of wall where the person had paused. The teen is too young to remember the Berlin Wall properly, but has been told by his parents of the city's former state of division.

The boy picks up the item off the ground that the hooded person had left behind. The teen can immediately tell by its shape and its passport-sized photo that it is an identification card. He knows enough English to be able to read at the top of the ID:

"SECRET INTELLIGENCE SERVICE
– MICHAEL DAVIES."

Get Your Free Copy
of "Murder at the Inn"

Don't forget to grab your free copy of Penelope Sotheby's first novella *Murder At The Inn* while you still can.

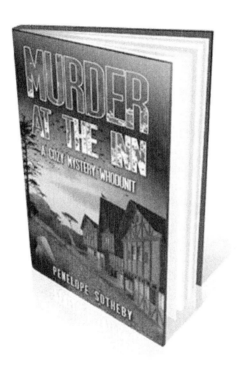

Other Books By This Author

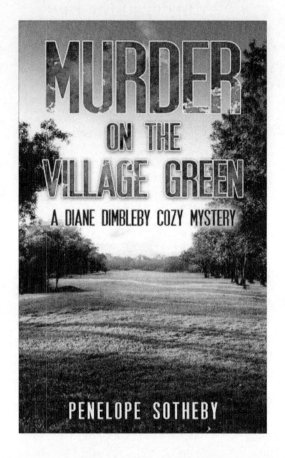

Murder on the Village Green

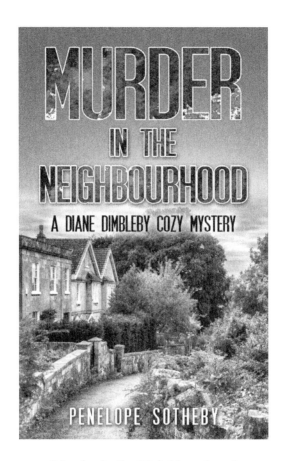

Murder in the Neighbourhood

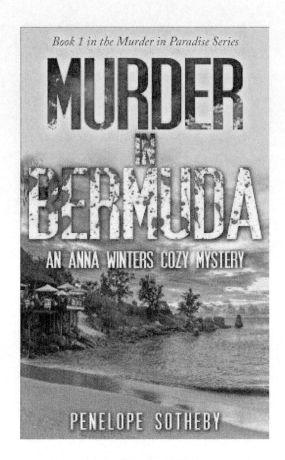

Book 1 in the Murder in Paradise Series

MURDER IN BERMUDA

AN ANNA WINTERS COZY MYSTERY

PENELOPE SOTHEBY

Murder in Bermuda

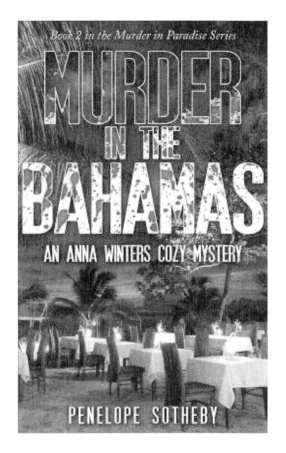

Murder in the Bahamas

Murder in Jamaica

Book 4 in the Murder in Paradise Series

MURDER IN BARBADOS

AN ANNA WINTERS COZY MYSTERY

PENELOPE SOTHEBY

Murder in Barbados

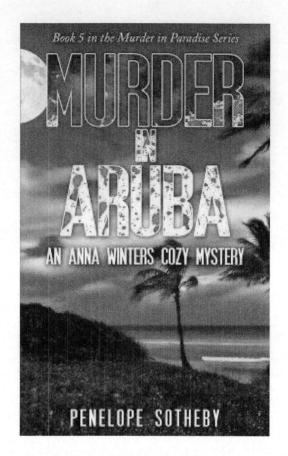

Murder in Aruba

About The Author

For many, the thought of childhood conjures images of hopscotch games in quiet neighbourhoods, and sticky visits to the local sweet shop. For Penelope Sotheby, childhood meant bathing in Bermuda, jiving in Jamaica and exploring a string of strange and exotic British territories with her nomadic family. New friends would come and go, but her constant companion was an old, battered collection of Agatha Christie novels that filled her hours with intrigue and wonder.

Penelope would go on to read every single one of Christie's sixty-six novels—multiple times—and so was born a love of suspense than can be found in Sotheby's own works today.

In 2011 the author debuted with *"Murder at the Inn"*, a whodunit novella set on Graham Island off the West Coast of Canada. After receiving positive acclaim, Sotheby went on to write the series *"Murder in Paradise"*; five novels following the antics of a wedding planner navigating nuptials (and crime scenes) in the tropical locations of Sotheby's formative years.

An avid gardener, proud mother, and passionate host of Murder Mystery weekends, Sotheby can often be found at her large oak table, gleefully plotting the demise of her friends, tricky twists and grand reveals.

Fantastic Fiction

Fantastic Fiction publishes short reads that feature stories in a series of five or more books. Specializing in genres such as Mystery, Thriller, Fantasy and Sci Fi, our novels are exciting and put our readers at the edge of their seats.

Each of our novellas range around 20,000 words each and are perfect for short afternoon reads. Most of the stories published through Fantastic Fiction are escapist fiction and allow readers to indulge in their imagination through well written, powerful and descriptive stories.

Why Fiction?

At Fantastic Fiction, we believe that life doesn't get much better than kicking back and reading a gripping piece of fiction. We are passionate about supporting independent writers and believe that the world should have access to this incredible works of fiction. Through our store we provide a diverse range of fiction that is sure to satisfy.

Printed in Great Britain
by Amazon